Simple Machines

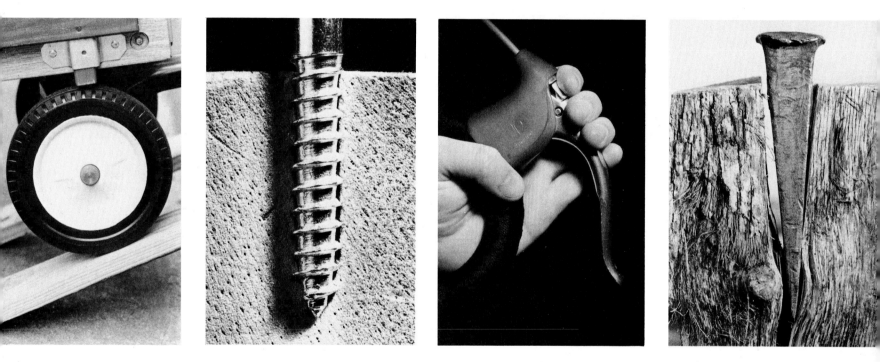

BY Anne Horvatic

PHOTOGRAPHS BY Stephen Bruner

E. P. DUTTON ▪ NEW YORK

What is a simple machine? You see simple machines every day, but you probably don't notice them. You use them too, but you probably don't realize it. You can find simple machines in places you might never expect.

- the ax your mom or dad uses to chop wood
- the wheels on your wagon
- the vise on a woodworking bench
- the steps you play on in the park
- the seesaw at the playground

All of these are simple machines. They don't need electricity to work. You make them work.

They are very simple. Sometimes you can see them working together in other machines. But they also work all by themselves.

There are five kinds of simple machines.

▪ wheel

■ inclined plane

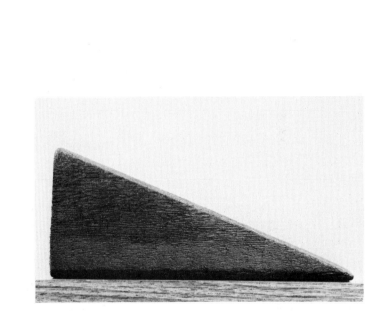

■ wedge

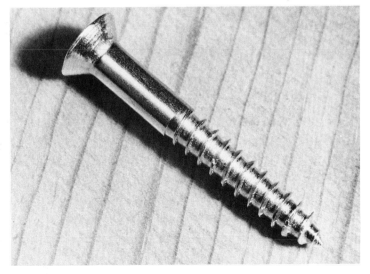

■ screw

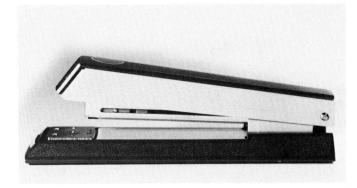

■ lever

All of these pictures show levers. Levers help us do many things. The brake handle on a bike, the stick used to pry the lid off a paint can, and the hammer claw that pulls out a nail are alike.

Can you see how?

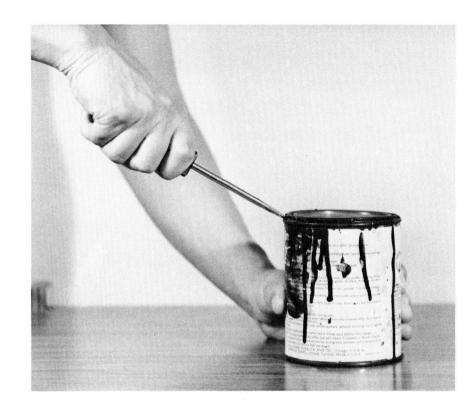

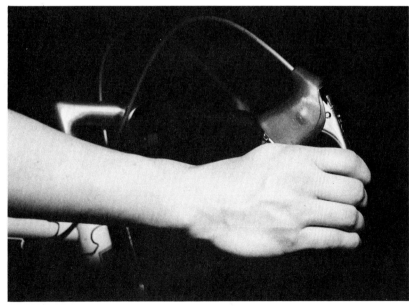

Someone or something must push or pull on a lever to make it work. Scientists have a name for this pushing or pulling. They call it force.

Think how you would pry open the lid on a can of paint. When you put a stick under the rim of the lid and push down on the end, you're supplying force to the end under the lid. That force pulls or pries up the lid.

When you open a can of soda, the same thing happens. Your finger pulls up the loop to push in the tab.

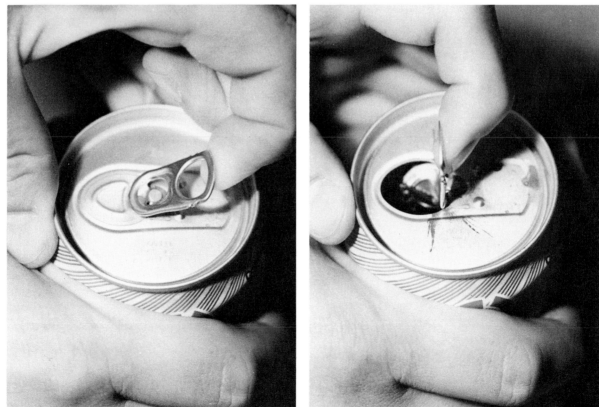

You can try this experiment in the park with a friend. Find a seesaw. Sit on one end, and have your friend sit on the other. Take turns going up and down. Think about what happens as you move. When you push yourself up, the force pulls your friend down.

If you weigh more than your friend, it's harder for your friend to hold you up in the air. But if you slide closer to the middle of the seesaw, what happens? It becomes easier for your friend to hold you up.

The reason for this is that you are closer to the fulcrum. This is the place that supports the lever.

All levers need support to work. The place where the seesaw rests, or is supported, on the bar is the fulcrum. The fulcrum doesn't move.

The farther the force is from the fulcrum, the easier it is to work the lever.

Can you find the fulcrum for each lever in these pictures? They show a person removing a nail with his hand near the hammerhead, someone opening a can of soup with her fingers near the top of the can opener, and someone squeezing a bicycle brake near where it connects to the handlebar. Try to do these things the same way. Can you do them? It's very hard. You'd have to be a superhero!

If you slide your hand farther away from the fulcrum and then use force to work the lever, you will find it is much easier to do the job.

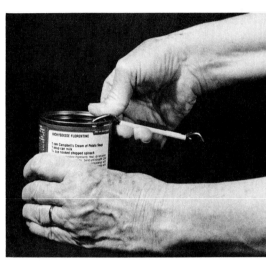

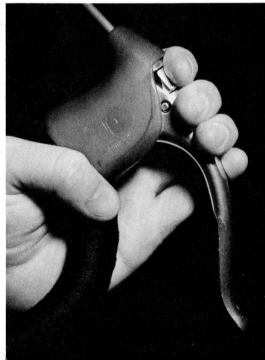

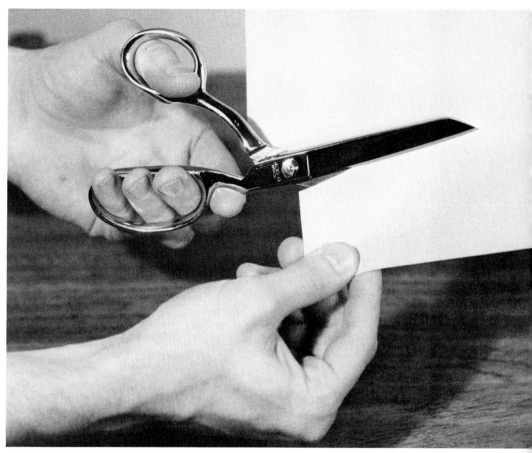

Levers have many uses. It's hard to think how we would do these things, and many others, if we didn't have levers.

Wheels are another kind of simple machine.
Wheels are all around us, too.
Like levers, wheels help us do many things.
They make our work and play easier.

Try to imagine what life would be like without wheels.

This load is hard to move. As the wagon is pulled along, the bottom rubs and drags against the surface of the ground. The heavier the load, the harder it is to pull.

If it is dragged far enough, the bottom of the wagon will wear down. This rubbing together of two surfaces is called friction.

There is a way to move a heavy load more easily, or with less friction. Place a long, round object, like a dowel or broom handle, underneath the front of the wagon. When the wagon is pulled, it rolls over the dowel. Because the dowel is round, it moves more smoothly and makes less friction.

A wheel works almost the same way as the dowel. Look closely at this picture of a wheelbarrow.

Now look at the wheel. It is round, like the dowel. But instead of rolling along under the wagon, the wheel turns around an axle. The axle is in the center of the wheel. All wheels need an axle, just as all levers need a fulcrum, to work. Like the fulcrum, the axle doesn't move.

All wheels move. Some wheels help us move.

Some wheels help us move things.

Some wheels help other wheels move.

In this picture of a bicycle, you can see that the back wheel is attached to a chain, which is then attached to the pedals. When someone pedals the bicycle, the chain takes the force, or energy, and makes the wheel move. The faster the bike is pedaled, the faster the wheel turns!

An inclined plane is a simple machine you see every day. It is a *very* simple machine.

In these pictures, you can see different rooftops. A roof has a flat surface. Scientists call a flat surface a plane.

These rooftops also slant or tilt. This is called an incline. The inclined plane on your house helps to keep rain and snow from collecting. The rain and snow easily run off the tilted surface.

Look at this picture of a ramp. Can you see how this is like a roof? It is a tilted surface. Like wheels, ramps help us move things more easily.

Steps are also inclined planes. They help us move from a lower level to a higher level.

People use either stairs or ramps to walk up and down, but usually ramps are used to move big loads. It's much easier to pull a load along a ramp than to pull it up and over a curb. A ramp is longer than a curb, so you don't need to use as much force to move your load.

Instead of the steps you see below, imagine a ramp to walk up. It would be very hard to walk up this ramp. It would be very steep. Steps cut a little space into the incline to make it easier for us to use.

Inclined planes are used in many different ways by lots of people.

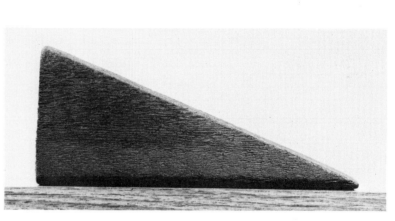

A wedge looks like an inclined plane, but it works differently.

A wedge uses force to come between two things. This happens three different ways.

A wedge tightens.

A wedge secures or holds.

A wedge splits.

A nail is a wedge that secures or connects one piece of wood to another surface (like another piece of wood or a wall). You use force to put the nail in place.

Sometimes a wedge uses force to split things. An iron wedge is driven into a log to separate it into two pieces. An ax uses force the same way.

Even your teeth can act like a wedge. When you bite into a larger piece of food, like an apple, you're splitting the food, making it mouth-sized to eat!

Sometimes a wedge fits between two things to hold them tightly. A wedge under a door fills in the space between the bottom of the door and the floor, to keep the door from moving. The door is held tightly.

The last simple machine is the screw. A screw begins to work much like a nail: It holds two things together. But instead of using force to hammer straight down, you turn a screw into the wood.

The screw has ridges around its shaft. The ridges are called threads. These threads cut a groove inside the hole as you turn the screw with a screwdriver. This makes the screw hold very tightly. To remove a screw, you need to turn it around the other way with the screwdriver. It's almost impossible to pull a screw straight out of wood or plaster or other hard material.

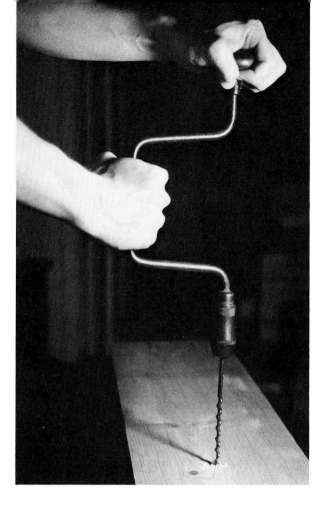

A drill works and looks like a screw, but it does a different job. A drill uses the thread to cut a hole. As you turn the drill, wood chips are carried around and around the thread path, up and out of the hole you are making.

The path the wood chips travel on is an inclined plane!

Have you ever tried to climb up a spiral slide? A spiral slide is like a drill. As you climb the slide from the bottom to the top, you're doing the same thing the wood chips do as the drill makes a hole. The wood chips move up a path to the top, just like you!

Some screws hold things together. Other screws move things along their thread path.

A grain grinder works like a drill. To use this machine, you turn a crank. As you turn, the wheat berries are carried along a spiral thread path to the crushing wheels.

Another screw and nut hold the crushing wheels together to grind the wheat berries into flour once they reach the end of the thread path. The tighter you make the screw and nut, the closer together the crushing wheels become, and the more force you'll need to use to grind the hard berries into flour.

Two kinds of simple machines work together in the grain grinder —the screw and the wheel.

Many tools we use are made up of several simple machines working together. A wheelbarrow gets its name from its front wheel. The wheel helps to move the load around. But when you lift the wheelbarrow to empty the load, the wheelbarrow is working as a lever. The wheel becomes the fulcrum!

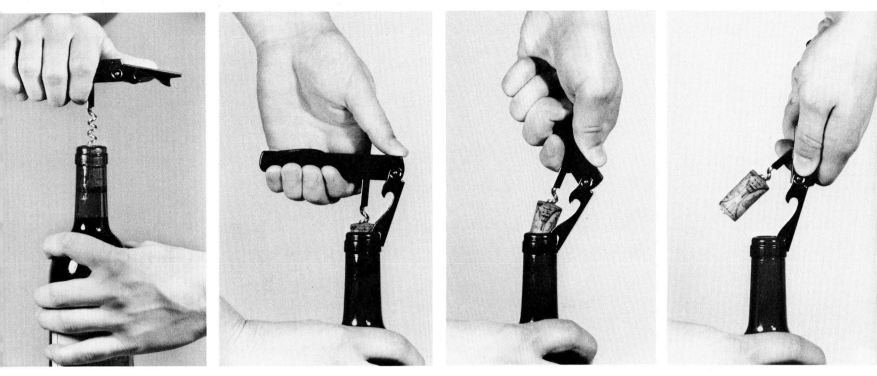

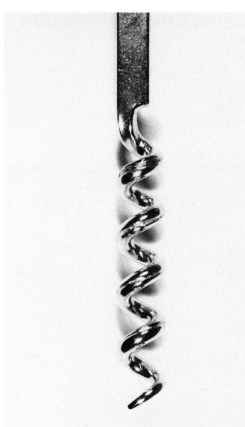

A wine-bottle opener, or cork-screw, uses a screw to go into a cork. Then a lever fits onto the lip of the bottle so the cork can easily be pulled out.

Look around you. Simple machines help us do many different kinds of work.

to my parents, Tom and Rita Horvatic,
and to the memory of my brother, Tommy ▪ A.E.H.

for Marylynn, Melissa, and Paige ▪ S.B.

Library of Congress Cataloging-in-Publication Data
Horvatic, Anne.
   Simple machines/by Anne Horvatic; photographs
by Stephen Bruner.—1st ed.
       p.   cm.
   Summary: Describes the five simple machines—
lever, wheel, inclined plane, screw, and wedge—
and explains how they work.
   ISBN 0-525-44492-0
   1. Simple machines—Juvenile literature.
[1. Simple machines. 2. Machinery.]
I. Bruner, Stephen, ill. II. Title.   88-29997
TJ147.H68 1989   CIP
531'.8—dc19   AC
Published in the United States by
E. P. Dutton, New York, N.Y.,
a division of Penguin Books USA Inc.
Published simultaneously in Canada by
Fitzhenry & Whiteside Limited, Toronto
Designer: Alice Lee Groton
Printed in the U.S.A.   First Edition   10 9 8 7 6 5 4 3